FIRST GRADE!
LET SCHOOL BEGIN

Inspiring Motivational Stories about Feelings, Courage, and Friendship
for the Start of Elementary School

Lisette Walter & Sabrina Hanslian
Illustrated by: Khayala Aliyeva

Pro Famalia
—VERLAG—

This book belongs to:

_____

Contents

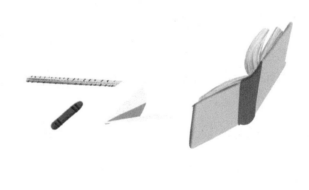

Introduction

The time in kindergarten is almost over and something new and exciting is about to begin: first grade!

You have made friends in kindergarten and had lots of singing, dancing, and fun with them. Now you are about to start elementary school. Your heart must be pounding because of your first day at elementary school. Your parents, grandparents, brothers and sisters are probably just as excited as you are. Your parents are also very proud because their little child has suddenly grown up so much that he or she is already going to elementary school.

Your first day at elementary school will certainly be a very big experience for you. On the first day, you will meet your new teacher and see your new classmates for the first time. Maybe you already know someone from kindergarten or a child from your neighborhood who is in the same class as you. Sometimes you find a new best friend in the first few days. You see your classroom for the first time and get your first timetable.

You have probably already gone shopping for a backpack with your mom and dad or grandma and grandpa—and soon you will have it on your back and feel really special.

The beginning of the first grade can bring up many

feelings. Maybe you are a little sad that you will not see your kindergarten friends every day, or maybe you are a little afraid that you will not find any new ones. You may also be nervous about whether you can write, read, and do math as well as the other children. Just be who you are and do not pretend for others. They will love you for who you are—and you will see how quickly you make new friends and how much fun you will have learning at school.

The little girls and boys in the stories feel the same way as you. The stories will encourage you as you start the new school year, and you will see that everything will be great!

Have fun at school!

Of Noodles and Friends

Leon was sitting in the painting corner of the kindergarten classroom. Next to him sat Kimmy and Ben. It was no wonder, because wherever Leon was, there was Kimmy, and where Kimmy was, there was Ben. Always. They were close friends, with matching wristbands and special handshakes. "A real gang!" Mom once said.

Suddenly Miss Jenkins, their teacher, said, "Leon, will you please come and get dressed? We are going to school today!" Leon stood up. Kimmy and Ben did too. Logically, because where Leon went, Kimmy and Ben went too. But not today. Today Miss Jenkins said, laughing, "No, you two, you will have to wait a little longer until you are big enough to go to the elementary school." Kimmy and Ben were irritated for a moment, but then went back to the group room.

Leon stayed behind alone. Not entirely alone, but with Miss Jenkins and a couple of children from the other groups, whom he did not know well and had already decided not to like. Children from other groups were strange, if only on principle. "But, Miss Jenkins, Kimmy is just as old as me. Why can't

she go to the first grade?" he attempted.

Miss Jenkins explained to him, "You will be six in August and Kimmy's birthday is not until two months later."

The group had to leave now. The whole way, Leon thought about why Kimmy could not go to the first grade. Could he do anything now that Kimmy could not? He thought about it for a long time, but the only thing he could do better than Kimmy was to pull noodles through his nose. He did not know for sure if Kimmy could do that. She just did not. She thought it was disgusting. He did not understand that, but they were still friends. There was no need to understand everything. Just as he was wondering why it was so important for pupils to pull noodles through their noses, they had already reached the bright red school building.

"Hey, little one, want to see what the big ones are doing?" someone called from one of the upper windows. Leon looked up at the window and saw Josh standing there. Josh is Leon's older brother. He felt terribly grown up right now because he was going into the fourth grade in the summer. Leon stuck his tongue out at him.

"What's he doing here anyway?" thought Leon. "Josh cannot pull noodles through his nose either. He must have cheated somewhere."

Leon would ask him about that at dinner. Maybe then he could tell Kimmy a trick for becoming a first grader too, without having to do anything disgusting. Leon's group pushed through a large, heavy glass door into a long, wide corridor. Colorful pictures hung on the walls and each door was a different color. There were many doors. It felt a bit like being in a rainbow. Leon liked the rainbow doors.

He was supposed to go through a green rainbow door with four other children of the group. Miss Jenkins did not go with them. That scared Leon. Other children were already behind the door—strange faces that Leon had never seen before. Although ... yes ... he had seen the adult at the big desk in front before. She told everyone her name, Ms. Miller, while a pair of large blue glasses with thick rims slipped off her nose. The glasses made her eyes look huge, like an owl. Leon had to laugh. Otherwise, everything was silent.

Leon laughed because of the picture of an owl in his head. The owl asked him to be quiet and listen. All

7

right, if the owl liked quiet, Leon would be quiet too. But that was difficult, because the owl (oh no, do not laugh!), in other words, Ms. Miller, talked a whole lot about starting elementary school and all the things they would learn together and that it was certainly great for the children to make lots of new friends.

Leon looked around. None of the children seemed to look like a new friend. They were all already talking between themselves. They did not need any new friendships. They already knew each other. Why did they all know each other, and he was all alone? He almost wanted to ask the boy next to him if he had ever shown someone how to pull noodles through their nose. But Leon did not dare.

Why could he not just bring all his old friends with

him? Leon was determined to practice the noodle trick with all the children in his group. There had to be someone who already knew how to do it. But suddenly there was a thud. Leon jumped up. Two seats over from him, a chair had fallen over. A girl with wild curls was just picking it up and angrily pushing it back to her table.

"Are you all right, Sina?" asked Ms. Miller.

The girl nodded at first, but then wiped aside a few curls that hung in front of her green eyes and said cautiously, "No harm done. I just do not like sitting around anymore."

Leon liked her immediately. Nevertheless, he was a little bit startled. Was he permitted to say something like that? Josh had told him there would be big trouble at school if you did not sit still and if you did not do as you were told. But Leon did not want Sina to get into trouble.

"I cannot sit any more either!" he suddenly heard himself say. Oh no, he had spoken faster than he would have liked, and he had also stood up. He would have liked to sit down again immediately. But it was too late for that now.

The owl smiled. "Do you two want to go outside for a while?" she asked. Sina and Leon looked at each other. Both nodded. "Alright but be back in ten minutes! There is a big clock in the schoolyard. Do you know when ten minutes are up?"

Sina knew it, but Leon was confused. "We are just supposed to go outside by ourselves? Don't you have to come with us, Ms. Miller?"

Again, the owl smiled. "What is your name? Ah, Leon...well, Leon, you are not alone. Mr. McConnell, the teacher's assistant, is outside."

Leon nodded, still a little unsure, then he ran outside after Sina. They climbed on the climbing frame for a while, and when Sina said, "I think ten minutes are up," they went back into the school building. Just outside the door, Leon could not stand it any longer because of his curiosity.

"Sina? Sina, it is totally awesome that you can also pull noodles through your nose."

Sina laughed and looked at Leon quizzically. "How do you know that?" she asked.

"Well, I thought all pupils had to be able to do that!" Leon explained to her.

Now Sina laughed even more. "It has nothing to do with noodles. You are really funny, Leon. Do you want to be friends?" That is what Leon wanted, and now Sina was his first new friend.

Reflection and comprehension questions regarding the first story:

- How does Leon feel when he goes to elementary school for the first time without his best friends, Kimmy and Ben? How would you feel?

- Why does Leon feel alone among the many children at school?

- What is the name of the "owl"? Do you think Leon means harm when he calls his teacher "the owl"?

- Why is Leon helping Sina? What would you have done in his place?

- What does Leon think of the idea of playing in the school playground without an adult?

- What do noodles have to do with pupils?

That Is Me!

Ever since Sina had returned to kindergarten classroom from the visit to the school, she had had a stomachache. Sina sat all alone on the plush sofa in the cuddle corner and kept her arms wrapped around her stomach.

Suddenly, there was a soft knock at the door. Sina was startled for a moment, but it was only Grandma, and it was nice that Grandma had come! Sina forgot for a moment that she had a stomachache, jumping up and falling around Granny's neck. "I do not believe this! What are you doing here in kindergarten?" said Sina.

Grandma laughed her great grandma laugh and lifted Sina high into the air. "Have you forgotten what we are going to do today?" asked Grandma. Sina thought about it. Then she remembered.

"We are going shopping for a backpack today," Sina answered in a pitiful voice. Grandma could hardly believe her ears.

"What is wrong my little mouse? You were so excited to choose a fancy backpack!" said Grandma. She now looked genuinely worried. Sina did not want that.

"Yes, of course. Backpacks are great. Let's go!" Sina shouted quickly and tried to smile, but she did not quite succeed.

In the meantime, Ms. Smith, Sina's teacher, had come into the room. Ms. Smith said to Grandma, "Sina is rather tired and has been complaining about a stomachache since the trip to school this morning."

"Okay, I will see how she is doing," Grandma said thoughtfully. Then Grandma and Sina left the kindergarten.

"Do you want ice cream later?" asked Grandma as the two arrived at the car. "Yeah, sure!" exclaimed Sina, beaming. Grandma smiled, knowing now that Sina did not have a real stomachache.

They drove towards the city. Sina sat on the children's seat that Grandma always had in the car. "I always have to take one of you children somewhere," she had explained to Sina. Grandma had eight grandchildren, so that was somehow true. The seat was lower than the one Sina always sat on with mom. She felt quite small.

At the traffic lights, Grandma asked, "I almost forgot. How was your trip to the elementary school?"

Sina stared intently at the door handle. "Oh, the..." Grandma waited for a moment and then she added, "Was it exciting? Did you get to know your teacher?"

Sina just shrugged her shoulders, mumbling. The car stopped. Grandma helped Sina out of the car. "And the other children?" Grandma kept trying.

"One, Leon, was quite nice. The others... they..." Sina fought it with all her might, but it was already too late. A big tear rolled down her cheek. At first it was just a droplet, but before she knew it, it became a whole torrent and Sina found herself crying

in Grandma's arms. For quite a while the tears would not stop.

When the tears had dried, Sina could speak. She talked about how the other children had laughed at her because she had fallen over with the stupid chair. She did not even know why the thing suddenly did not want to stay next to the table.

"Oh dear—did the teacher scold you?", Grandma wanted to know. But she had not. The woman with the big glasses had allowed her to take a short break. That had been cool at first. But afterwards, when Ms. Smith had collected the children so they could go back to the kindergarten together, Jonah had snitched and said that Sina had behaved very stupidly.

The children had laughed at Sina again and Sophie had said, "Well, if you cannot even color without getting your hands dirty and do not know how to do pigtails properly, you do not belong in elementary school anyway."

Grandma felt sorry for her. The children had not been very nice to Sina. But before Grandma could think about how to help Sina, Sina jumped excitedly onto a small wall next to the parking lot and announced, "Grandma, I have it! You are a doctor. Doctors are terribly clever. You just teach me to read and do arithmetic really quickly. Then I will be able to do it much better than everyone else and no one will say I am stupid!"

Grandma tilted her head and said nothing. Sina was confused. "What is the matter, Grandma? I can do this...for sure! You don't think I am too stupid for this too, do you?" Sina's eyes widened in horror. She had not expected that from her grandma.

Although Sina was now stamping her foot angrily on the ground and ranting about how unfair everyone was, Grandma stroked her hair and smiled her grandma smile again, though a little worriedly. "Bad case of 'oblivious,'" she then commented. It sounded like a disease.

Sina audibly drew in air through the gap in her teeth. "Is that dangerous?"

Grandma bobbed her head a little. "We will see what we can do." That did sound pretty bad now.

For a while, they walked side by side in silence. Sina knew the way to the bookstore, which also sold the backpacks. She liked the store. But now Grandma stopped at a completely different shop window. All the fancy dresses were on display. "Which one would you like for your first grade enrollment?" she wanted to know from Sina.

"The girls in my group would all wear those," Sina replied, pointing to a festive pink dress.

"And if you would wish for a special friend for school, what would she like to wear?"

Sina laughed, "Some funny colorful tights with animals on, and jeans shorts."

"I see..." said Grandma. "What would the girl in the colorful tights be like?"

Sina did not think about it for long. "Well, she would play and climb wildly with me and have great ideas all the time. And she would not laugh at others. I am sure no one would say that she is stupid."

They walked a little further and reached the big bookstore with the backpacks. There were lots of toys at the entrance. "Do you find anything interesting here, Sina? You are welcome to look around!" Grandma invited Sina to linger awhile.

"The other children all collect cards like those there and they are totally crazy about colorful pens that somehow smell like melon."

Grandma looked skeptically at the melon pens. "I see. Does the girl in the colorful tights also like melon pens?"

Sina shook her head. "No, she likes things you can really do something with." She pointed to a carving book for children.

"I see..." said Grandma again. "Would you like to try this too?" Sina wanted it. They took the book to the second floor where the backpacks were.

Each backpack was part of a big set, with a pencil case, a pouch, a sports bag, a drinking bottle and a

lunch box. Sina was amazed to see all the things a pupil needed. "Which one would you like?" asked Grandma. Sina thought about it. "At school, Melly says these mice are really great, everyone wants them."

"I see...", Grandma said. "And your friend, who likes carving so much, would she also like pink mice?"

"No," Sina answered and laughed. "She would think the turquoise backpack with the silver—ball is totally cool."

"I see..." Grandma said again. Sina tried the turquoise bag with the silver soccer ball on. She liked it so much that she immediately kept it on, on her way down to the checkout.

On the escalator, Sina got all excited and tugged Grandma's sleeve. "Grandma, look," she whispered, and pointed to the mirror next to the escalator. "That is me, and I look just like the friend I would like to have!"

Sina was wearing colorful tights and jeans. Her red curls fell untamed onto her face, and in her hands, painted with a felt-tip pen, she held a carving book in her hands On her back, she carried a turquoise backpack with a dazzling soccer ball on it. "Wow, I look totally cool... And kind of cute and..."

Grandma understood and pulled Sina back to the mirror. Sina looked at her reflection again and said confidently "That strong girl, that is me!"

Reflection and comprehension questions for the second story:

- Would Sina like to go on an excursion with Grandma? What did they have planned for today?

- Why does Sina not want Grandma to be worried about her?

- Why does Grandma ask Sina if she likes ice cream?

- How does Sina feel sitting on the seat in Grandma's car? Is it possible that she never noticed this before? Why is it different today?

- Why is Sina crying? When was the last time you cried?

- Why does Sina think she has to learn a lot very quickly?

- Sina talks a lot about what the other children like. Do you have any idea why she does not say what she likes herself?

- What do you think of Sina's friend with the colorful tights?

Elementary School Enrollment with Obstacles

Jonah woke up because he heard a garbage truck outside his window. Tired, he dragged himself out of the bunk bed and closed the window to block out the street noise. His pajamas stuck to his stomach. He was all sweaty from the sultry summer night. The sun was brightly shining on him from the veranda. Sleepily, he watched the garbage men at work. The alarm clock showed seven o'clock. Why hadn't anyone woken him up? Was it the weekend? No, it wasn't weekend! His favorite TV show was yesterday. It was always on Thursday. So, it had to be Friday. But someone was rattling the cups in the kitchen.

Jonah wanted to crawl back into his bunk bed. Halfway up the ladder, it hit him like lightning. Today was no normal Friday; this was his first day at elementary school. Grandma and Grandpa would be coming soon and then they would all go over to the school together. The beautiful new backpack stood packed in the hallway, just waiting to be claimed by its new owner. Jonah almost fell off the ladder with excitement. Like the wind, he dashed into the kitchen.

"Daddy!" Dad was standing at the cookstove, dressed only in pajama bottoms, frying eggs. "Good morning, big boy!" he called, grabbing the excitedly bouncing Jonah. Just in time, mom was able to push the pan handle aside. Jonah almost hurled the frying pan off the cookstove. Her cheeks were all red. Jonah always thought that was very pretty.

"Well, are you happy, little one?" she said and hugged Jonah tightly. Then she told him to go to the bathroom and get ready.

While Jonah was still brushing his teeth, the doorbell rang. He heard Grandpa's voice in the hallway. Like a rocket, the child's toothbrush flew back into its cup and Jonah tumbled out of the bathroom into the hallway.

"There is our first grader," his deep voice boomed through the hallway. Then he mumbled something about, "Your last day of freedom!" which Jonah did not understand. But it did not matter—he could hardly keep still or pay much attention to anything because of his excitement anyway.

He barely noticed what he was eating while he devoured his breakfast. It was only when mom frantically started searching through his wardrobe that he really got back on track. "What are you doing? Is something missing?" Jonah asked cautiously. Cautious, because he knew that mom often forgot something on days like this and this was a little worrying.

Mom said, "No, everything's okay," but she did not exactly look like "everything's okay."

"Fraaank!" she shouted, upset. Dad joined them in the children's room. "Frank, look!" said mom now in panic, pointing at Jonah. Jonah was busy buttoning up his new suit pants. That was quite difficult. Was it so important that Dad had to come right in?

"Oh," said Dad in the tone he used when he did not want mom to get upset, but when it was already too late for that.

Jonah asked uneasily, "Now what?" Adults were sometimes pretty stupid.

"Your pants are too short..." Dad remarked with a grin, which completely upset mom. She continued to rummage through the wardrobe for a pair of pants that would fit, ranting wildly. Jonah looked in the mirror. Sure enough, the smart suit pants they had bought in May, especially for the first day of elementary school, now did not even reach his ankles. That is why he could not zip them up. It was not his fault at all.

"I'll just go in a different pair of pants then." Jonah did not know whether to be proud of having grown like this or to suspect a problem.

Mom actually could not find any "normal" pants without a pattern or hole at the knee. They finally decided on a pair of black pants with a red patch. Mom reluctantly admitted that the black pants worked quite well with the black jacket. The problem was solved.

Finally, the whole family was at the front door in their almost best clothes. Jonah was happily hopping around them again. The pants incident had been forgotten.

Just then, Dad came around the corner with the great turquoise backpack they had picked out from the catalogue. Jonah slumped a little under its weight. Oh dear, he also swayed when he walked, but did not want anyone to see. He was big now, after all! When Grandma shed a little tear because she was so touched by her big boy, he almost exploded with pride himself. He felt liked he had grown another five centimeters in height and proudly presented the bag on his back.

They went the short route to school on foot. Jonah always walked ahead. Grandma and Grandpa should see that he knew his way around. He had practiced the path with Mom and Dad over and over again during the summer. Nevertheless, everything looked different today, brighter and more colorful. All the people seemed to be happy for him. Even the mail man wished him all the best for his first day at elementary school.

When he arrived at school, Jonah preferred to walk between his mom and granddad. There were so many people here, he could hardly believe it. The whole schoolyard was full of nicely dressed moms, dads, grandmas, and grandpas, with a comparatively small crowd of little schoolchildren with big, brand-new backpacks in between. The children were being constantly reminded not to get dirty and not to run away.

Jonah's family lived in a small town. Therefore, Jonah recognized many faces in the crowd. The girl with the red hair, who had made so much fuss the other day when they had visited the school, was standing not far away from him. Today she did not look so strange. She even had the same backpack on her back as Jonah. She was nice, after all. Jonah waved to his friends from kindergarten.

Tobi came running straight towards him and they greeted each other with their usual Native American roar. The boys were about to show each other their new backpacks when it happened. Tobi spun around a little bit too fast with the unaccustomed weight on his back and hit Jonah in the face with his schoolbag with full force. Suddenly there was a little bit of blood on his white shirt. The adults standing around went completely out of their minds. From all sides, handkerchiefs were handed out and concerned questions were asked. A toddler started crying, and Tobi's mom even wanted to call an ambulance.

Everyone was quite upset.

All except Jonah. Jonah was sitting on the floor, grinning like a Cheshire cat in his blood-stained white shirt. In his raised hand, he held a small treasure and shouted, "Finally, you have done it, Tobi. My wiggle tooth  is out!" Tobi and the other children were immediately thrilled.

"Awesome! Cool! I want to see it too!" Jonah heroically showed his tooth around while the adults held their bellies in laughter.

However, no one had noticed the two women who were standing at the school gate to call the children together. Only now did one of them make her way through the crowd. She wore thick blue glasses on her nose and a boy, who Jonah thought was called Leon, whispered loudly, "Oh look out—the owl!"

The children laughed, and the parents looked embarrassed. Leon tried not to attract attention, and Jonah's mom took a wet wipe out of her handbag, with which she attempted to make her child presentable again. The attempt was futile, but a woman in the crowd (a girl's mom—Jonah knew her from the nursery) offered a spare shirt, a pink glittery one with a colorful unicorn on the chest. Jonah screwed up his face, but what could he do? The owl, whose name Jonah could not remember at all, now insisted that all the children should go into the school building.

Later, on the big class photo that was to hang on the wall next to the blackboard for the whole school year, Jonah was seen proudly holding a turquoise backpack into the camera, wonderfully color-coordinated with his pink unicorn shirt and patched pants. His grin was as wide as ever, just a little incomplete. No one had minded, not even mom.

- Jonah was very tired when the garbage truck awakened him from his sleep. Why was he, nevertheless, wide awake so quickly?

- Why is Jonah's mom more forgetful than usual on special days? Are you sometimes too?

- Were the parents angry with Jonah because the suit pants would not button up easily?

- Why shouldn't anyone see that Jonah was swaying a little under the weight of his backpack? Are you also looking forward to carrying your backpack?

- Why does the route to school seem particularly colorful and bright to Jonah today?

- Why do all the adults suddenly get "upset" and what does this expression mean?

- Did something bad happen to Jonah? Why does he suddenly need a new t-shirt?

My Words, your Words

Emma stood a little bit apart from the others, half hidden, next to the climbing frame at the far end of the schoolyard. A little enviously, she watched many people greeting each other and talking about trivial things. Waiting, they kept glancing at the clock on the school tower. What Emma was waiting for, she did not know exactly.

The children were all going to elementary school for the first time today. They were the same age as Emma. It was their first grade enrollment. At home, Emma had already spent two years learning to read and write.

Nevertheless, it had been nice to go shopping for school together with her new mom and Tobi, and she was also looking forward to the barbecue tonight. Tobi was her new brother, and he was also going to elementary school for the first time. His whole family would be coming for a visit later. Emma was already looking forward to seeing them, because it was a bit like her family now that Dad had married the new mom. That her own grandma was not coming made Emma a little sad. However, she could understand that it was too expensive to fly from Europe to America just for a few days. It was much better if Grandma stayed with them for several weeks in the winter.

But what was not good at all was that Tobi seemed to have completely forgotten about her. He had promised her rock-solid that he would stay with her if she did not understand something, and now he was skipping through the crowd with a kindergarten friend up ahead, not even looking for her behind him.

The crowd now started to move. A woman was obviously calling the children together. Emma certainly had to join them. Reluctantly, she dropped the leaf she had been kneading in her hands the whole time and ran to the group of children. It was not so easy to squeeze through all the perfume-and aftershave-scented  adults. Everyone was crowded around the entrance to get a good look at the new elementary school class.

When Emma finally fought her way through, she quickly moved to stand next to Tobi. Some of the other children laughed and pointed at her. What had she done wrong again? The teacher said something.

Emma thought she heard the word for "girl." Then she realized her mistake: there were two rows of children, one for girls and one for boys. Emma was standing with the boys. How embarrassing! She quickly rushed to the other side.

Tobi said, "Sorry I did not take care of you." They ran up a flight of stairs, through a green door and into the first-grade classroom.

The teacher talked a lot and Emma understood a little bit. Finally, Ms. Miller read a story. Now Emma understood a little bit more.

After a while, Emma realized that she urgently needed to use the bathroom, and she had no idea where the restrooms were in this huge building. Tobi certainly knew. Emma's eyes searched the room. Tobi was sitting in the back corner near a closet, and she was sitting in the front next to the window near the teacher's desk. Emma began to play nervously with the ribbon on her dress. Maybe it would not be long before they could leave.

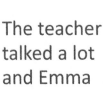

Ms. Miller read and read. Emma had meanwhile pulled the ribbon completely out of her dress. Luckily, it was only decoration. Where had the words gone? She had taken an extra English course with her dad and now she could not even ask where the restrooms were. This was not a good start. Nothing helped; she made a brave attempt and addressed the boy next to her in broken English: "You help? I go restroom. How go?" He obviously did not understand a word. Helplessly, she repeated her question in German. "Could you please tell me where the restrooms are?" The boy seemed honestly helpful, but now he understood even less. This was going to be disastrous. How was she ever going to connect with anyone like this?

Just then, someone tapped Emma on the shoulder from behind. "Are you looking for the restrooms?" Emma could hardly believe her luck.

"Yes, would you help me?"

"Of course." The girl raised her hand, spoke briefly to the now non-reading teacher, and then led Emma to the restrooms.

Washing her hands, Emma took a closer look at the other girl. The girl's name was Lina. When she laughed, her white teeth sparkled like stars from her dark face with its dark black hair. She wore a multicolored dress that looked so different from the dresses of the other girls. It looked more festive, had rich colors with colorful embroidery patterns. To Emma, Lina looked almost like a princess.

"Are you from somewhere else, too?" asked Emma in German as she tried to release one of the paper towels from the dispenser. Lina rolled her eyes and blew a foam soap bubble off the back of her hand. "That is what everyone thinks. But I was born in Boston! Mom and Dad used to work in Boston."

Emma wondered, "Then why do you speak such good German?" Lina now began to free towels from the dispenser as well. They pulled together and suddenly the whole clump of paper towels loosened from the holder. Snorting with laughter, they tried to stuff the sheets back in.

"That is complicated. Well, not really. Mom speaks

German at home. Mom is from Bremen. Dad met her there once on vacation. Mom's parents are from India. My grandma lives in India, but we cannot visit her until next year. Papa says flying is so expensive."

Emma knew that from somewhere. "Could you teach me to speak two languages too?" asked Emma.

Lina frowned. "I do not know. I did not learn it at all. It just happened, I guess. I am sure it will work for you too."

Later, as the children walked through the big school gate back to their parents, they beamed with pride. Emma, however, was beaming the most. Now she was really enjoying her elementary school enrollment. Her shyness of trying out the new language was completely forgotten.

Reflection and comprehension questions for the fourth story:

- Have you ever been to another country where no one knew your language? How did it make you feel?

- Would it be awful for you to see your grandma

only once or twice a year? How would you stay in touch? Maybe write letters or talk on the phone?

- Have you ever learned words in a foreign language? Was that difficult for you?

- Could you imagine going to school in a foreign country? How would you feel?

- Can you tell which country people come from by their appearance?

- Do you have to speak in the same language to be friends with other people?

- Emma could write numbers and letters before she started school. Are you also able to do that?

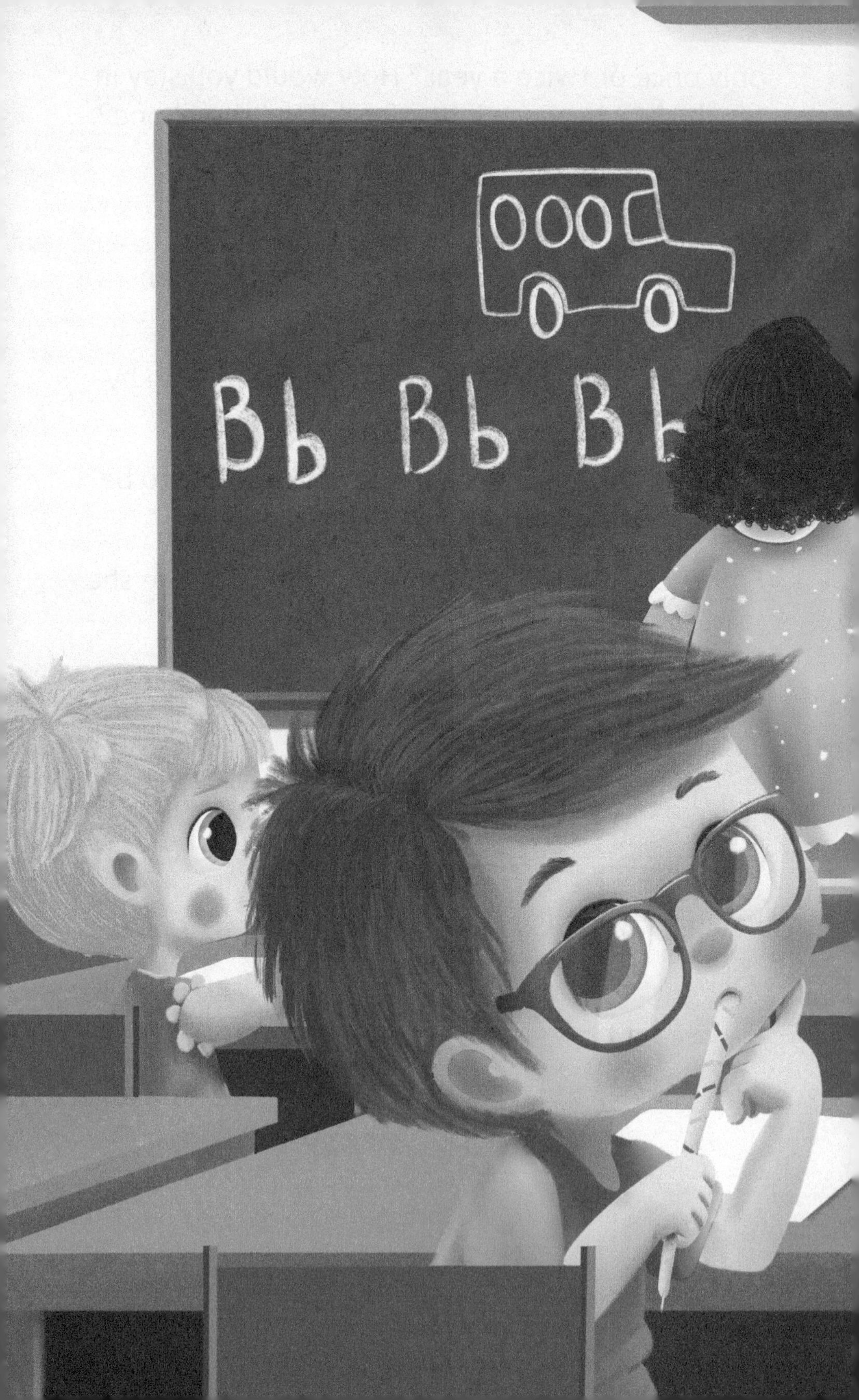
Вь Вь

My Rat Must Be with Me

It was nine o'clock in the morning. The first elementary school class sat quiet as mice in their classroom. New books were laid open on the tables in front of the children. Each child had a sharp pencil in his or her hand, ready to immediately copy every stroke that Ms. Miller would write on the white board.

Finn also had a pencil in his hand, but he couldn't concentrate on writing. He stared out of the window. Dark clouds blocked the view of the sun. Thick raindrops trailed across the dusty windowpanes.

Ms. Miller spoke of bears, bread, bobbles and buses and drew a letter on the blackboard that looked to Finn more like a three with a dash. He suppressed a yawn and let his head sink onto his arms. His gaze wandered absently around the class. Almost everyone was listening intently. Leon and Sina were secretly swapping football cards in the back row. If Ms. Miller would have seen that! A glance to the front, however, showed Finn that it was very unlikely that she saw anything at all. Ms. Miller was now struggling with the projector, which she was trying to convince there was a movie to be shown on the whiteboard.

From the corner of his eye, Finn noticed a movement. Laura's backpack was on the floor next to Laura's chair and sure enough, Laura's bag appeared to be

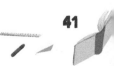

moving. On Laura's bag was a picture of a pink mouse. Finn sat upright so that he could see better. A tiny pink nose poking out of the zipper. The fluffy little nose slid tentatively over the edge of the backpack.

Long, nervously twitching whiskers, two red beady eyes, round little ears and lots of white fur followed. The white fur gathered on the edge of a schoolbook and headed towards Laura's desk. A mouse! No, more like a rat! Finn wanted to warn Laura, but he was too stunned to interrupt the scene that was unfolding before his eyes.

The white rat pushed itself up and heaved its little fluffy bottom onto Laura's table. Sniffing, it looked around for a few seconds and then headed straight for the girl. To Finn's amazement, Laura did not cry out in fear, but whispered, "I told you to stay in there, Toffee!" and held out her hand to the rat. The rat continued to look around and then slowly wiggled towards the hand. From there it flitted quickly up onto Laura's shoulder, where it took a seat on its hind legs and began to brush its round cheeks as a matter of course. Laura seemed completely unimpressed and turned her gaze back to the whiteboard, where a movie had just started about colored monsters singing about bristles, boards, beans and balloons. Finn's mouth remained open in astonishment.

The silence did not last for long, because of course

the relatively large animal did not remain unnoticed by the other children. "A rat!" Sophie shouted angrily and chaos broke out.

For Finn, everything seemed to happen at once. Several pupils jumped on their chairs; others squealed. The rat got the fright of its life and rushed towards the windowsill. This made Laura lose her temper. She shouted, "No, Toffee, not out of the window!" and pursued the rat.

Since she was nowhere near as dexterous as the animal, she tore several books and pencil cases off the tables as she ran. The chaos hit Leon so suddenly that he even let the football cards, which he had just been holding in his hand, fly across the room. Only Ms. Miller did nothing. She stared dumbfounded into the room while the monsters continued to sing about bees, bratwurst and blackberries.

Sina finally put an end to the chaos by decisively jumping forward, grabbing the fleeing rat with a firm grip. Toffee did not seem happy about the abrupt end to his wild adventure, but calmly let himself be handed over to his little owner. Since the danger had apparently been

eliminated, the class calmed down and Ms. Miller found her words again. "Laura? Is that your rat? You cannot just bring an animal to school!"

Laura contorted her face in annoyance and replied a good deal too loudly, "That is not just any animal, that is my best friend Toffee. If Toffee can't come, I do not want to come either. Toffee always goes with me wherever I go!" The rat started brushing its long whiskers and made a few squeaking rat noises.

The class thought this was very cute and everyone said, "Oh" and "Ah" except Ms. Miller. "We cannot do that, Laura; we are going to have to take the rat back to your house now."

That hit a sore point. Laura got angry and even started stamping her feet. Finn looked up in surprise. He had been gathering cards from the floor with Leon until just now. "If Toffee's going, I am going too!" shouted Laura, causing the rat to almost flee again.

Ms. Miller looked genuinely astonished. "Laura, that is not the way we do it!"

Laura snorted. "But Toffee like me and that is why Toffee is staying!"

To the delight of the audience, Sina now joins in the discussion. "That is so freaky! Your best friend is a rat. Cool. How did you teach Toffee to stay with you all the time?"

Laura had not been expecting that. In her bewilderment, she almost forgot to be angry. "I did not," she answered truthfully. "Toffee just likes me." Everyone found that impressive, except Ms. Miller, who was looking for her smartphone.

"Does Toffee like grapes?" asked Sina, already holding her lunch box in her hands. But Laura did not have to answer. Toffee immediately reached out to Sina with curiosity and grabbed the grape without hesitation.

The class thought
this was awesome!

Laura grinned and
declared, "If you
have food, you are
Toffee's friend and
whoever is Toffee's
friend is my friend
too!"

To everyone's
delight, the rat was
now calmly eating
the fourth grape. Only Ms. Miller still did not share
this enthusiasm. She adjusted her large glasses and
disappeared from the room with her smartphone.

"Well," Leon said, laughing, "Maybe owls do not like
rats after all." Finn laughed with the others. Who
would have thought that an hour full of bags, balls,
blades and branches would be so exciting?

Reflection and comprehension questions for the fifth
story:

- Can you listen quietly even though you do not feel
  like it?

- What do you think would have happened if Ms.
  Miller had caught the children exchanging football
  cards in the back row?

- Would you have watched the rat appear as calmly as Finn did? Do you like rats and mice?

- Do you have a pet too? Do you think it would be allowed to visit you at school?

- Would you have had the courage, like Sina, to stand by a friend in a dispute with the teacher?

- What would you have done if you had been sitting in that classroom?

- Would Laura get into trouble if Ms. Miller called her home? What would your parents have said?

- Would you have found a lesson on letters as boring as Finn or do you enjoy learning something new?

Not Everyone Can Do Everything

The school bell called the children back to the classroom from the break. An unusual sight awaited them there. Ms. Miller had arranged the tables, which were usually placed in a large U, into one big worktable. In the middle of it stood a basket of fruit and kitchen utensils such as boards, lemon squeezers, small knives and large spoons.

"Sit down" urged Ms. Miller, smiling to the pupils rushing in. "Everyone take a board and then we will count all the fruit together for a big fruit salad."

Josi screwed up her face. "Spinach? I hate spinach!"

Sina laughed. She pointed to the big bowl and exclaimed, "No, those are the leaves from the tangerines!"

Now Josi was grinning too. "I like tangerines."

Not all the children shared this opinion, but they were still curious. After a few minutes they were all sitting around the table expectantly.

"Have any of you never cut fruit before?" asked Ms. Miller. No one came forward. Ms. Miller seemed relieved. "Let us divide up the fruit then. Sina? Please take a lemon." Sina took a lemon from the large fruit basket in the middle of the table. "Do you know what

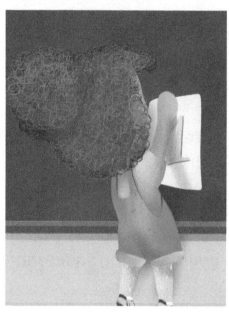

the number one looks like?" asked Ms. Miller. Sina nodded and took a lemon from the large fruit basket in the middle of the table.

"Good, then pick out a picture of a big one here and pin it to the board!"

There were several colorful little cards in front of Ms. Miller. Sina knew that they all represented numbers, even if she could not name them all. She recognized the one and pinned it to the board. It was just as yellow as the lemon in her hands.

"All right, now Laura is going to take two apples," said Ms. Miller. Laura stood up and took two apples. But she did not know what a written number two looked like. That was no big deal. Ms. Miller simply showed her which the right card for the blackboard was. So, it went on with Ben and three pears, Finn and four tangerines, all the way up to Josi. "And Josi take the banana and cut it into ten pieces!" Josi took the banana,

cut ten pieces and looked for the number ten on the table.

After Josi, it was Emma's turn. Emma was excited. She had not quite understood everything because she still did not speak English very well, but she certainly knew how to count. She waited eagerly for Ms. Miller to take her turn with the eleven. But Ms. Miller surprised her and asked her instead if she could recount all the numbers up to ten. This amazed Emma—not only because she was given a completely different task but also because she understood everything immediately. She proudly counted from one to ten in English and then she was allowed to start the exercise  all over again with a lemon. Paul took two apples. Jonah three pears and so on, until Lina was left with only ten pieces of banana.

Finally, the children began to cut their fruits into small pieces. Most of them did it very well, and in no time at all they had a bright fruit salad. The children were in a good mood and when the dishes had been cleared away and the table wiped, Ms. Miller asked Josi to fill two small bowls with fruit salad. Josi immediately began to scoop eagerly, but she filled ten bowls.

"Oh Josi, stop!" said Ms. Miller kindly. "You were only supposed to fill two bowls."

Josi shrugged her shoulders in amazement. "I did— ten bowls!"

Ms. Miller held up two fingers. "Two, one for you and one for your neighbor. But just pass on the other bowls; after all, everyone should get one."

During the meal, the children were allowed to talk freely. It was nice, like a big picnic in the classroom. Josi also had fun. She sat between Leon and Sina and talked to them about football techniques. Then

Finn called out to her, "Here, give this to Sina!" and handed her a big glass of water.

Josi took the glass and carried it to Lina. She looked at her and did not know what to do with the glass. Then Sina called out to her, "Come here, that glass was for me!"

Josi blushed and took the glass to Sina. Sina thought for a moment. "You do not hear well sometimes, do you? Lina and Sina sound the same. Like two and ten."

Josi blushed even more then. "Yes, I am quite hard of hearing," she said quietly, so that only Sina would hear her.

But Leon had heard her too. "Sina, why don't you say it?" he said without thinking.

"But I don't want everyone to know!" Josi answered annoyed.

Sina put a reassuring hand on her arm. "But if you are hard of hearing, how else can you hear me anyway? I have not noticed anything yet."

Josi lifted her hair from her ears. The children saw two small hearing aids stuck behind her ears. "I see," Sina said, fascinated. By now everyone was listening. "But it is still easier for you if we know that you cannot hear everything. Then we will just say things twice." Josi did not seem to be very happy with that.

Ms. Miller understood. "It is great that you still participate so well and learn so quickly! That must be doubly exhausting. It is exciting how some people compensate for such a challenge. I have a pupil in the fourth grade who is almost blind, but she always knows exactly where her things are and even has a favorite color. She says she can feel differences in her fingertips. And Max in the third grade has so much strength in his arms that he even plays basketball in his wheelchair. I am curious to know how you do it. How do you help yourself when you do not get it quite right?"

Josi wrinkled her forehead and thought about it. "Often, I can see what people say, how Sina's mouth moves, what she points to when she talks. Are there really that many kids here who are different?"

Before Ms. Miller could say anything in reply, Sina interjected, "Josi, you are not different! You are just like the rest of us. Some things you're great at, other things you're not so good at. That is quite normal. Not everyone can do everything."

Reflection and comprehension questions for the sixth story:

- Would you like to make a big fruit salad together with many other children? Have you ever made something like this before?

- Do you cook at home with your family from time to time? Do you already know how to cut with a vegetable knife?

- Why is Ms. Miller relieved when she finds out that all the children have already cut fruit?

- Would you have already found the picture for each number from one to ten? Why does it not matter whether the children already know all the numbers or not?

- Would you enjoy a classroom picnic?

- Were you surprised that Josi cannot hear well?

- Do you know people with similar challenges as Josi, Max or the girl in the fourth grade? How do these children help themselves in everyday life?

- Could you imagine addressing such a situation as openly as Josi and Leon are doing in the story?

Of Art and Skills

Lunch had just finished. The pupils cleared up the last plates and then they went to the silent work. Jonah was also supposed to go, but he was nowhere to be seen. Leon stopped nervously at the door to the canteen. The two boys had become good friends since they'd started the first grade together. Of course, Leon did not want to leave his friend behind now. But not going to the silent work would mean trouble. What should he do?

Indecisively, he stood around in the schoolyard and cracked a chestnut with his shoes. Then he heard a dragging sound coming towards him. Jonah ran across the schoolyard, his face red from the exertion. The backpack dragged carelessly, pulled by a strap, on the ground behind him. "Jonah, where have you been? You missed lunch and now we are going to be late for the silent work," Leon told his friend.

They both ran the rest

of the way. While gasping, Leon explained, "I left my pencil case in the music room. I wanted to get it back quickly, but I couldn't find the room. Everything looks the same here! Then I found the room, but I took the music book instead of the pencil case and had to go back again." Leon did not quite understand it all, but that did not matter.

Luckily, there was no supervising teacher yet in the room when they entered the class. They both quickly went to their seats and took their workbooks out of their backpacks. While Leon started with math, Jonah tried hard to open his pencil case. The clasp was stuck. Finally, it came loose with a tug. But it happened rather suddenly, and the contents of the pencil case flew across the room. Just at that moment, Mr. Morgan stepped through the door.

"My goodness Jonah, why don't you put the pencils in the loops properly? Then this would not happen." He grumbled and went to the teacher's desk where the first pupils were already waiting with questions about their homework.

Jonah saw Sina frowning at the chaos near their seat and his face turned dark red. He muttered, "Sorry!" Sina helped him to collect the pencils.

Finally, everything was in place and Jonah had found the right page in the workbook (thanks to a hint from Sina). He was happy. Now he could draw numbers. That was easy. Today it was the turn of the six. One row of big sixes, one row of small sixes—that will be easy. He grabbed a green pencil and was ready to start.

Then Emma and Lina two rows back began to giggle violently. Jonah thought that Emma and Lina were laughing at him. He dropped the pencil and then decided to pick another color. Blue sixes. They looked nice, three blue sixes, four blue sixes—as blue as the kite Jonah had made with Dad, a really rich blue. He wanted to try it out this afternoon if the weather stayed like this. You needed wind to fly a kite...Oh no, what was that? Something was wrong with the second row of blue sixes. Jonah narrowed his eyes. They were wrong. He had written nines by mistake. How had that happened?

He searched frantically for an eraser. But he could

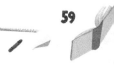

not erase the blue. He tried it with a squirt from his water bottle and created a blue lake in his book. Jonah was getting more and more upset. He could not hand it in like that. The noise in the room grew louder and louder. Two children were quarreled over a hole punch Another one opened a bottle of sparkling water with a loud "fizz." A lost bee buzzed at the window. How was

anyone supposed to know what they were doing in this chaos? Angrily, Jonah folded his workbook shut.

"You have finished already?" This question came promptly from the teacher's desk. Jonah opened his workbook again, but he did not want to do sixes anymore. He preferred to draw a nice big dragon on his sheet. In between, he watched Sina practicing letters for the English lesson. Maybe he should ask Leon if he wanted to play soccer today. But what if his parents have something else planned for this afternoon? Did he not have something planned for himself? Oh yes, the blue dragon! Then he remembered that he had forgotten all about the sixes.

Jonah concentrated and had just picked out the blue pencil again when Mr. Morgan suddenly stood right in front of his desk. In shock, Jonah dragged the pencil he had just picked up, right across his paper. Mr. Morgan smiled. "Jonah, tell me, are you alright?" Jonah nodded. "Hmm…" said Mr. Morgan, "I have a feeling you've forgotten how to do your homework. Would you like me to show you how to write a six again?"

Jonah almost cried, it made him so sad. "I can write a six, I know I can! I can write really great sixes, but it is so noisy in here! I have to look somewhere else all the time. Someone is always distracting me. Here no one can write well. I cannot do anything. I am like the ultimate idiot!" he complained and puffed, glaring at the other children. In his opinion, it was their fault that Mr. Morgan thought he could not solve the simple tasks.

Mr. Morgan was now distracted himself. "Jonah, did you draw this?" he asked, pointing to Jonah's sheet. "That is great!"

The children craned their necks to look at Jonah's sheet. There was really something to see. A big fire-breathing dragon. He was sitting next to a castle overflowing with treasures. But the treasures were made of honey, and around the honey buzzed a row of bees. It was a picture as sharp as something out of a picture book, only not quite colored yet.

"Wow. Will you make me one of those? That is so beautiful!" one of the children shouted, and the other children were talking in a jumble. It was only one sheet. He had hundreds of them at home.

"I like to paint," he said cautiously. Mr. Morgan laughed in amazement and asked the children to be

quiet. They sat down again.

"Jonah, you are really good at this. You are an artist, and we did not even know it. I am going to talk to Ms. Miller straight away. She is looking for someone to draw posters for a school project. Would you be interested in helping her out a bit?"

Jonah nodded, but still found nothing special about it. He was a little embarrassed by the way everyone was looking at him.

Sina grinned. "I would be proud if I could do that!" she said.

"Really?" asked Jonah, feeling a little flattered now.

"But writing the same nice six for a long time, I still cannot do that," he said, again visibly annoyed. That is when Mr. Morgan had an idea.

"If the other children's conversations bother you, you can just turn them off." He reached into a drawer of the classroom cupboard and pulled out large headphones without wires.

"It would not be any better if I listened to music on top of it all," Jonah grumbled.

"You won't hear any music. You will not hear anything," Mr. Morgan reassured him.

Jonah tried out the headphones. Silence? Well, at least almost. He could still hear a murmur. But it was far away. He made another attempt and indeed, by the end of the silent work time, he had nicely drawn all the rows of sixes. He almost did not notice the others jumping up to go to their work groups. During playtime, his friends came up to him to see his picture again. Now Jonah was a little proud of his talent after all.

Reflection and comprehension questions for the seventh story:

- Why did Leon wait for his friend Jonah after lunch, even though he had to go to the silent work? Would you have done the same for your friend?

- Something is always going wrong for Jonah! Do you sometimes feel the same? How does it feel for you when nothing works the way it should?

- When was the last time you had trouble concentrating on something?

- What do you do if you cannot concentrate properly?

- What do you think of when you see a beautiful

shade of blue?

- Would the headphones like the ones Jonah got in the story help you too, or would they bother you?

- Do you like painting as much as Jonah in the story? What do you like in particular?

May the Better Team Win

Finn stood in the equipment shed with a soccer ball in his hand and did not know what to do. In fact, he was hiding by the shadow of the front door. The ball had to be put into the ball container before the end of the break. The ball container was next to the pedal cars, just to the right of the jump ropes. Finn knew his way around here by now; the children got their toys from the equipment shed next to the gym at every break. None of this was a problem.

But the fourth-grade boys next to the ball container were a problem. Finn was terrified of these guys. The blond one with freckles, Sven, always pushed the smaller children when they squeezed through the entrance door after the bell. The one next to him, a boy with a cap and a boxer nose, Elliot, had taken the last pudding from him in the canteen the other day and then whispered in a nasty tone, "You better not tell, or we will have a fight!"

Finn had widened his eyes and marched silently back to his table. He had never noticed the third one before. But when he was with the other two, he was probably just as mean.

The doorbell rang in the background. Now Finn had to get out of here somehow. He took a deep breath in and out. Like a weasel he dashed to the soccer balls, threw the soccer ball into the container and wanted to get out again immediately, but Elliot had already recognized him.

"Oh look, a midget! Scared to be alone in the dark?" he sneered, blocking his way to the door.

"Let me out," Finn hissed, now no longer afraid but already quite angry.

"Why? What are you going to do if I just stand here?" the big boy asked challengingly. Finn snorted. He did not know.

Then the third big boy spoke up, "Now leave him alone. We have to go in too."

"Are you as much of a weakling now, Josh? If you like, you can mess with me right now!"

Josh raised his eyebrows threateningly. He did not like Elliot. "At least you will have an equally strong opponent and not some little child who does not even come up to your chin. That is cowardly!" he returned.

Finn did not want any of them to support him. For him, they all belonged together. Besides, he was not a midget. "I am much better than him!" he shouted, turning to Josh. He continued saying to Elliot: "I have seen how you play soccer. You dribble like a beginner!"

While he was speaking, a large shadow fell on Finn's face as if coming out of nowhere. Mr. Morgan, his gym teacher, was now standing in front of them. This man was so tall that hardly any light penetrated through the door frame into the equipment shed next to him. Finn did not know if he should be relieved or if he now had an even greater problem. "Elliot! Josh! Sven! I have had enough. Can't you leave the little ones alone? Josh really—you are the class president; you should know better."

All three were silent. Josh muttered something like, "I tried!" but so quietly that he could hardly be heard. Finn peered past Mr. Morgan. Good that Mr. Morgan was on his side.

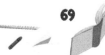

Behind Mr. Morgan at the door, he saw Leon from his class. He seemed to have called the teacher. Finn immediately felt more courageous with his friend nearby. "That is right, and if you do not, we will show you how strong we are. You only feel better because you  are taller! But wait, we are much more skillful, and we are not as stupid as you." Finn was now literally overwhelmed by his anger. He was not small at all. And why should he submit to such a mean boy?

For Elliot, this was too much. He felt humiliated by Finn. How dare such a wretch speak to him like that? Mr. Morgan stepped in between and pushed the fighting boys far apart.

"Enough!" announced Mr. Morgan in a sharp tone. "We are going to end these silly arguments after silent work time once and for all time! Elliot and Finn, each of you will be outside the gym at two o'clock sharp with ten other children from your year group. We are playing soccer. A nice sports competition. Do we understand each other?"

The children looked at each other, puzzled. Josh and Leon looked embarrassed. They were siblings after all. They did not want to fight against each other. But Josh winked at his little brother. "I already have an idea!"

And indeed, at 2 o'clock, two groups of pupils met at the soccer-field. On the right, under the big chestnut tree, six scowling fourth graders were waiting. On the left, at the tool shed, were eleven excitedly giggling first graders. Josh was waiting in the middle.

"Hey, come over here! Nice of you to join us!" Elliot now called out in an incredibly friendly manner.

But Josh shook his head. "After you were so mean to me earlier, I am not playing with you after all. I am here to cheer on my little brother, just like the others." In fact, he had offered to referee for Mr. Morgan. However, he did not want to reveal that to Elliot just yet.

At that moment, several fourth-grade girls came across the schoolyard, chatting and joining Josh. Melly with her red curls waved cheerfully to her sister Sina from the first grade. "After all, we do not want you to think we are all like them!" she shouted, pointing her chin at Elliot and the boys next to him.

Elliot turned a little pale. "That is complete treachery, isn't it? We are in the same class, after all!" he indignantly shouted.

"Yes," Mr. Morgan's voice shouted from the front door. "Children who you insult will not side with you,

Elliot. Any more of you coming?"

Elliot grumbled, so Sven replied, "No, there are not that many of us boys in the fourth grade and half of them have tennis lessons now and did not want to skip it."

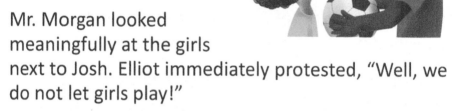

Mr. Morgan looked meaningfully at the girls next to Josh. Elliot immediately protested, "Well, we do not let girls play!"

"Then it is your own fault!" Sina snapped, and so it happened. The mixed team of the eleven first graders was far superior to the six fourth graders. The latter shot hard and accurately, but hardly coordinated themselves and had to withdraw one of their teammates after the first half because of a foul. Josh and Lina worked as referees. The first grade won 5:2. At the final whistle, the children were in each other's arms as if they had just won the Champions League. Finn was happy. Not only had they won, even though they were much smaller, they had won together. He realized that all these children—Jonah, Sina, Ben, Tobi, Leon and the others—no longer just went to the same class with him, but that they had now become friends. Friends who could count on each other.

Reflection questions and comprehension questions for the eighth story:

- Have you ever been bullied by a bigger child for no reason? How did you feel in that moment?

- What did you do to help yourself in that situation?

- What other possibilities would there have been to solve such a problem?

- Have you ever made someone angry for no reason? How did you feel afterwards? Did you feel sorry for the other person?

- Do you think it was right for Leon to call a teacher?

- Why does Finn manage to get a soccer team together without any problems and Elliot does not?

- How many children played soccer?

- Do all the children in a group or class always have to be friends with each other?

A Halloween Excursion

There had been a lot of excitement in the whole school for days. The Halloween festivities were about to begin! Each class was allowed to organize this day as a project day. There were no lessons. Everyone was allowed to dress up and to do something exciting together. Ms. Miller had also thought of something nice for her pupils. Dressed up, they wanted to take a hike through the forest and to have a ghost party inside the old ruins. The morning remained free, and the excursion took place in the afternoon so that the ghosts could meet at dusk.

Lina and Emma were ready and waiting at the gate to Laura's garden for their friend to finally come out. Sina was dressed up as a witch with a long nose and green fingernails. Emma was a werewolf with fur and plush ears. But Laura was dawdling. "Come on, Laura. We are going to be late!" cried Lina impatiently. "In a minute," came the reply down from

Laura's room.

"There you are!" Lina said. Instead of Laura, Leon, Finn and Jonah had turned up. The three boys were also wearing scary costumes.

"What a creepy vampire!" exclaimed Sina giggling when she saw Leon.

"Don't you think Frankenstein's monster and the mummy are scary too?" the other two wanted to know right away.

When Laura joined them, the contest of the scariest costume was underway. The ghost princess, who Laura played very convincingly, stopped the contest and the children hurried to get to the schoolyard on time.

There, the rest of the creepy little monsters that the first graders had turned into were waiting. Only Amin was missing. Amin was a rather shy boy whom everyone liked but who never really got noticed. If Ms. Miller had not had her list, she would have forgotten about him. The wild crowd was already shouldering their backpacks when Amin finally turned around the corner holding his father's hand.

Amin was dressed up as a cat. A cute cat, with bushy fur and a pink nose. "I am sorry. Amin did not like his first costume. We had to start all over again!" his father said apologizing.

"Wizards are so stupid, Dad," Amin affirmed. Then he looked around and directly hid two steps behind his dad's broad shoulders. Were those pupils actually the other children from his class? They looked terrible! The zombie there had blood on his neck and the witch had huge black eyes. The vampire had a red streak dripping down his chin and one of the girls had a third eye painted on her forehead. It all looked pretty disgusting to Amin. But they laughed convincingly as usual. Why did they like to be repulsive?

"Amin, do not worry about this. When you are eating sweets, it does not matter what you look like," Leon shouted. He grabbed his friend by the hand to pull him along with the others. It was the secret hope of all the children to be able to eat mountains of sweets at the Halloween buffet in the ruins. Amin was not excluded from this either, so the group finally set off.

In rows of two, the children started the one-hour walk from the school to the ruins. It was exciting to walk all together through the streets. They chatted and joked around. At the intersections, Ms. Miller always went out into the street first and stopped the traffic with her arms outstretched. The drivers then had to stop, and all eighteen children crossed the road waving happily.

Arriving at the forest, there was a surprise for the children. Ms. Miller opened her large bag that she was carrying and handed out a small torch for everyone. "So that we can find our way in the dark," she said. Only now did the children notice that it was already dusk. Fog was drifting through the almost bare trees, and it was drizzling a little. Ms. Miller turns on the torches, and the children became very quiet.

The last thousand five hundred feet were exhausting—it was steep uphill. When an owl called, Sophie involuntarily let out a little scream. The others laughed nervously. "Just an owl," Frankenstein's monster said a little uncertainly.

The moon began to shimmer through the branches and the moths circled around the little torches. Lina stared, entranced at the crazy animals, so fascinated by the warm light that they burnt their little wings on the glow of the fire. Then something hissed past her face, "Whoosh." She held her breath in shock. The others were also startled and stopped. There were flutters everywhere.

The ghost princess was the first to recover and exclaimed: "Bats, it is a whole swarm! We must have scared them!" Indeed. Lifting their torches, a little up to the sky, they saw a whole swarm of little animals fluttering through the air.

"Freaky!" commented Leon.

"Creepy though," Amin agreed. No one objected. Finally, they reached the ruins.

Surprisingly, there was some light up here. The children ran towards the entrance with curiosity. There were lots of their moms and dads, some dressed up, some not. While the children were on their walk, they had transformed this little ruin into a veritable castle of magic. Colorful lanterns hung from the crumbling walls. There were artificial spider webs at the small windows and spooky bones and magic books were scattered everywhere.

The children did not know where to look first! On the right side of the wall were tables with glittering tablecloths, on the left a buffet. Quickly, everyone grabbed a plate.

The buffet was incredibly crazy. Who had all these ideas? Their parents? A huge pumpkin was enthroned in the middle of the delicacies, cleverly carved into a wild grimace. Another one served as a large, fragrant soup bowl. Finger sausages lay on a silver tray and the salad was given a very special touch with glowing egg eyes. Rubber snakes and chocolate spiders lurked between cups and plates. The dessert had been turned into gooey slime. A large cucumber crocodile almost stole the show from a puff pastry dragon. The latter guarded magic wands made of salt sticks and other wild creations. The children could not eat so much spooky food, they could not try it all. Only Amin stood a little skeptically in front of a "bloody" red Jell-O and finally opted for a piece of bread with cheese. His nose wrinkled in horror as he watched Sina letting a chocolate spider crawl into her mouth. He thought it was disgusting. He did not like being scared.

After dinner, Jonah's dad positioned a small loudspeaker and everyone danced to funny party music until they came together, exhausted, in a large circle of cushions. It became quiet again and Ms. Miller took the floor. Her flushed cheeks could be seen in the flickering light. She too had been happily celebrating with parents and children and was now a little bit out of breath.

"You know what, it is lovely being with you all!" she said. The children clapped and shouted wildly that they had had a lot of fun too. Then Ms. Miller continued, "Now that we are all sitting together so comfortably, I would like to know: How do you like it in our school? Is everything as you expected?"

It was not so easy to get the children to speak one after the other. They all wanted to talk about their experiences at the same time.

"I thought I would never be able to learn anything

and now I can already read a little!" exclaimed Sina.

"It is so great to play with all of you, and yet I was afraid I would not make any friends at all. What nonsense!" said Jonah and laughed.

While Josi said, "Jonah drew so beautifully in my friend's book! Anyway, it is overflowing now because I have gotten so many nice entries."

Josi's comment was immediately confirmed by several children, and Emma was also pleased, saying, "I didn't think there would be such a great Halloween party this year.

Now a white flash shot out of Laura's hat and the children jumped up in fright. "Toffee, come back here at once!" Laura had indeed brought her rat with her. But in any case, it matched her witch costume. Tobi held his stomach while laughing. Only half a year ago, he would not have believed that school could be so exciting.

Reflection and comprehension questions for the ninth story:

- Have you ever celebrated Halloween? What did you like and dislike about it?

- Do you like scary costumes? How would you dress up?

- Why does Amin think some costumes are

"disgusting"? Do you think it is okay that Amin does not like being scared?

- What do you really find "disgusting" and why?

- The children walked with torches through the forest in the dark. Do you think you have to be particularly brave to do something like that? Have you ever been in the forest at night?

- Would you have been afraid of the bats or of the owl?

- Why is it scarier alone in the dark forest than together with friends?

- Would you have tried the strange Halloween food?

- At the Halloween celebration, children, teachers and parents danced wildly with each other. How does it feel for you to dance wildly with others?

Imprint:

Authors: Lisette Walter and Sabrina Hanslian

Translator: Nicolas Hepp

Editing/proofreading: Emily Hutchinson

Proofreading: Susan Keillor

Design/cover/illustrations: Khayala Aliyeva

Lisette Walter and Sabrina Hanslian

are represented by:

Oliver Hanslian

Wilhelm-Busch-Weg 9

28329 Bremen / Germany

Contact: info@famalia.de

Made in the USA
Monee, IL
06 July 2022

99139868R00050